Acting Edition

Thataway Jack

by John Rustan
& Frank Semerano

I0591799

ǁ SAMUEL FRENCH ǁ

ISBN 978-0-573-62526-8

www.concordtheatricals.com
www.concordtheatricals.co.uk

FOR PRODUCTION INQUIRIES

UNITED STATES AND CANADA
info@concordtheatricals.com
1-866-979-0447

UNITED KINGDOM AND EUROPE
licensing@concordtheatricals.co.uk
020-7054-7298

Each title is subject to availability from Concord Theatricals Corp., depending upon country of performance. Please be aware that *THATAWAY JACK* may not be licensed by Concord Theatricals Corp. in your territory. Professional and amateur producers should contact the nearest Concord Theatricals Corp. office or licensing partner to verify availability.

MUSIC AND THIRD-PARTY MATERIALS USE NOTE

IMPORTANT BILLING AND CREDIT REQUIREMENTS

An earlier version of THATAWAY JACK was given a workshop production at Occidental College in Los Angeles on April 24, 1986. The production was directed by Rusty Jones and featured the following cast:

PEVERAL SOMMERSET BIDDINGWELL ...... Scott Graff

THATAWAY JACK.......................... Kirk Graves

ELEANOR RAVENCROFT .... Lisa Carstens

AMBROSE RAVENCROFT................Jeremy Bishop

TALKING BOAR .... Marc Cardiff

FARGO CALLAHAN .... Jim McKeny

LUCY................................. Veronique Merrill

DERBY DAN TURNER..................... Ian Montone

The set was by Peter Ballenger, lighting by Toni Pogue and Heidi Van Kirk, costumes coordinated by Laurel Edgecomb, sound by Jeremy Bishop, stage managed by Karen Chu.

This version of THATAWAY JACK was first presented by The Colony at Studio Theatre Playhouse in Los Angeles on April 29, 1987. The production was directed by Bob Ari and featured the following cast:

PEVERAL SOMMERSET BIDDINGWELL... Nick DeGruccio

THATAWAY JACK .... Robert Budaska

ELEANOR RAVENCROFT.................. Lisa Beezley

AMBROSE RAVENCROFT .... Whitney Rydbeck

TALKING BOAR....................... Jonathan Palmer

FARGO CALLAHAN..................... Jeffrey Rockwell

LUCY............................... Bonita Friedericy

DERBY DAN TURNER .... Hugh Maguire

The set was by Todd Nielsen, lighting by Gary Christensen, music by Jeffrey Rockwell, costumes by Therese Lentz, stage managed by Carole Lineback.

The authors wish to thank
Omar Paxson, Ione Semerano, Bonita Friedericy

CAST OF CHARACTERS

PEVERAL SOMMERSET BIDDINGWELL — *A wayfaring young banker*

THATAWAY JACK — *A seasoned prairie man*

AMBROSE RAVENCROFT — *New and eager proprietor of the Laramie Inn, recently out from Cleveland*

ELEANOR RAVENCROFT — *His wife, and not-so-eager co-proprietor*

TALKING BOAR — *Faithful Indian companion to FARGO CALLAHAN*

FARGO CALLAHAN — *The Rhyming Cowboy. Legendary self-appointed upholder of law and order*

DERBY DAN TURNER — *The West's most notoriously mean and rotten outlaw*

LUCY — *PEVERAL'S mailorder fiancee*

SETTING

SCENE 1

Prologue. A campsite on the prairie three days outside Laramie

SCENE 2

The Laramie Inn

NOTE: The Prologue can be played in front of the main set, perhaps with a backdrop, and with only a few props.

TIME

The beginning of the end of the glorious days of the Old West

THATAWAY JACK

SCENE 1

SCENE: A campsite on the open prairie a couple of days ride outside Laramie.

TIME: Just before dawn.

AT RISE: PEVERAL SOMMERSET BIDDINGWELL, a young man in well-tailored city clothes, enters the campsite, which is momentarily deserted. HE approaches the campfire and pours himself a cup of coffee. As HE sits down with his coffee, HE looks forlornly around, unsure of what to do. HE takes a picture out of his breast pocket, looks at it and sighs. THATAWAY JACK, a grizzled man of the prairie enters and quietly puts a rifle to the back of PEVERAL'S head. PEVERAL, oblivious, puts the picture back, and takes a sip of his coffee. (NOTE: As with any character in this play, THATAWAY JACK is not a cariacture, though there may be something of the stereotype to him. THATAWAY JACK is robust, gritty, warm, sarcastic, and very real. His age can be anywhere from forty to sixty. He is in full possession of his faculties, he can see out of both eyes, and is not hard of hearing or otherwise physically impaired. He is, in fact, as strong as an ox.) As PEVERAL takes a sip of his coffee, THATAWAY speaks:

THATAWAY JACK. Good coffee?

PEVERAL. *(Turning around, startled.)* I'm sorry. I ... didn't know anyone was here.

THATAWAY JACK. I figured as much. No sudden movements now.

PEVERAL. I assure you, sir, you can put that rifle down. I'm just passing through.

THATAWAY JACK. I made me some good diggin's today, so if you don't mind I'll just keep this here mule-eared blaster pointed at yer head 'till yer all done passing through. What's yer name?

PEVERAL. Peveral Somerset Biddingwell.

THATAWAY JACK. Whoooaa! What say I beat it with a stick and make it "Pete." Man's gotta have a short handle on his name if'n he's gonna survive in rattler country.

PEVERAL. *(dejectedly)* You may call me what you wish. It no longer really matters anyway. Nothing matters, anymore.

THATAWAY JACK. *(cheerily)* Nothing matters! Well fine! You're just the one to help me finish off this stew, Pete. I call it outlaw stew. Tends to hold up inside you.

PEVERAL. *(As though he'd rather not.)* Please, if you don't mind...

THATAWAY JACK. Don't mind in the least. *(Pours out some stew, while keeping his rifle trained at PEVERAL. He hands the stew to PEVERAL who just looks at it.)* Go on, boy, use yer spoon. It ain't gonna sprout wings and fly in yer mouth!

PEVERAL. *(Cautiously taking a bite.)* Um ... delightful ... really.

THATAWAY JACK. Now don't let yer spoon set in there too long without movin' it about. Freeze right up on you.

(PEVERAL gives it a stir.) So, what you doin' out here? Why the long face?

PEVERAL. *(Looks at Thataway, sighs.)* Lucy.

THATAWAY JACK. Woman! I might 'a knowed it! Man's jaw don't drag on the ground 'less'n a woman's hanging onto his chin hairs.

PEVERAL. She was to be my bride. When I graduated from Fairhaven College I moved out west. Since I didn't know anyone I arranged to meet Lucy through the mail order bride service. We've been writing each other a year and a half. Suddenly she's decided she doesn't want to marry me any more. When I think about it, I guess that suits me fine.

THATAWAY JACK. Well, shouldn't oughta! Dan'el Boone, I think it was, once said, "All a man needs is a good gun, a good horse, and a good wife."

PEVERAL. Really?

THATAWAY JACK. Sure. The way I figure it, if you're looking for trouble, you got yer gun. If you found too much trouble, you got yer horse. And if you ain't got trouble enough, you got yer wife. Ha! Ha! Ha!

PEVERAL. Nothing personal, Mister...

THATAWAY JACK. Thataway Jack's the name.

PEVERAL. *(Scratching his ear.)* Well, nothing personal, but...

THATAWAY JACK. *(Bringing up his rifle.)* Easy, Pete. Almost lost your ear there.

PEVERAL. *(Slowly dropping his hand to his side.)* ...I think you've missed the point. Lucy isn't just a woman. She's a *lady*.

THATAWAY JACK. Ah Hell! I gone out with plenty of

ladies — down New Orleans way. Aluetta Rosebush was one. A real lady. Not a tattoo on her body — 'least none she would let you see without you first givin' her a big can of hickory nuts, and maybe some flowers. Yes sireee! A quality lady!

PEVERAL. *(Puts his hand in his shirt.)* Yes, but look...

THATAWAY JACK. *(Bringing up his rifle again.)* Pull it out *slow*, Pete. I may not be particular smart, but I knows me just enough letterin' and cipherin' to fill in your gravemarker.

PEVERAL. *(Slowly taking the picture out of his jacket.)* This is a picture Lucy sent me of herself. What more could any man want?

THATAWAY JACK. Well dress me up in chicken feathers and throw me to a lion, if she don't make you want to lick the thorns off a cactus!

PEVERAL. I never sent her a picture of myself. I was afraid she might be put off.

THATAWAY JACK. *(Looking him up and down.)* Yer smarter than I first give you credit fer, Pete. Where's this Lucy girl now?

PEVERAL. In her last letter to me, she said she was coming out here to meet her true hero. You see she'd been reading a great deal about the Wild West and got it into her head to come out and meet this man and ... well, to make a long story short, I took the first stage out of Denver to try and cut her off. There were no seats left so I had to ride on top with the luggage. We hit a bump, and I fell off. *(THATAWAY chuckles.)* I suppose it was foolish to begin with.

THATAWAY JACK. So you want to find Lucy before this

other feller does. What's his name?

PEVERAL. *(Indicates that he wants to get something out of his jacket pocket. THATAWAY nods.)* I've got it in the letter somewhere. *(Opening the letter, reads.)* Oh yes, here it is. Derby Dan Turner.

THATAWAY JACK. *(shocked)* DERBY DAN TURNER!!! Oh Pete, you done it now!

PEVERAL. What do you mean?

THATAWAY JACK. Oh my, oh my, you done it now. I tell you, Pete, you're the only man alive who could swallow a full-grown procupine and still have enough bad luck left over to get the hiccups.

PEVERAL. What are you trying to say?

THATAWAY JACK. I ain't never met Derby Dan, but I've heard tell plenty. He can't stand the thought his women ever wanted another man. What you gonna do?

PEVERAL. I was hoping to catch her before she met up with him. But ... I don't even know where I am. Could you help me find her?

THATAWAY JACK. I'm good, boy, real good. I can juggle five bobcats while fightin' off a Sioux attack. I use a bear trap for a pillow, and clean my teeth with barbed wire. But Derby Dan Turner? He's downright mean!

PEVERAL. Can you tell me how to get to a town called Laramie?

THATAWAY JACK. You mean yer still goin'? *(PEVERAL nods.)* I'll be straight out with you, Pete. This here situation's got less give than a fat lady's corset. It'll take a miracle, boy.

PEVERAL. A miracle. Thanks. *(Dejectedly starts to leave.)*

THATAWAY JACK. I swear Pete, you got enough open

range between your ears to file for statehood. Don't you get the point? The best miracle is them you make for yourself. Come on, let's go. *(Gets up and starts packing his things.)*

PEVERAL. You'll go with me?

THATAWAY JACK. I guess I could take you that far. Besides, I got me kind of a plan.

PEVERAL. Well, thanks, Thataway. How far is Laramie?

THATAWAY JACK. Oh, Laramie ain't fer a'tall. Let's see, we could go by way of the Shawnee trail.

PEVERAL. Sounds good. *(Starts picking up the coffee pot, etc.)*

THATAWAY JACK. 'Course you may not want to go.

PEVERAL. Why not?

THATAWAY JACK. It's got Shawnee on it.

PEVERAL. Oh. *(drops everything)*

THATAWAY JACK. There *is* the Chickapaw pass, and as I recollect they wouldn't mind.

PEVERAL. That's fine. *(picks up gear)* You're sure the Chickapaw wouldn't be any trouble?

THATAWAY JACK. Heck no. They ain't trouble to nobody since the Shawnee killed 'em all.

PEVERAL. *(drops the gear)* Shawnee again?

THATAWAY JACK. What do you want me to do, boy? Mail you in a box marked fragile? Conjure up a flood and throw you out in a bottle? This here is mountain country. You get by doing. Out here even the nightingales is mean. Why, a feller figures the lord is smiling down pretty on him if he climbs in his bedroll and only finds a dozen sidewinders a'waitin' fer him! I like you Pete, it's a fact that I do, but I think you're going through life tryin' to milk a dry cow. What I'm trying to say, Pete, is that your caboose ain't exactly hooked up to yer engine. To be plain...

PEVERAL. PLEASE! I'm just asking if perhaps there isn't an easier way to get to Laramie.

THATAWAY JACK. Ooooohhhh ... There *is* the Goodnight Lovin' Trail. Ain't no way to lose your scalp, neither. Just your self-respect. *(smiling)* There's a lot of quality ladies up thataway.

PEVERAL. How long will it take?

THATAWAY JACK. As long as I can make it take!

PEVERAL. Well, that's fine. Can we get started now?

THATAWAY JACK. Sure. Now you just walk ahead of me real slow Pete, and remember, if I see you go for anything other than a laugh, I'm gonna blow yer head off.

PEVERAL. You mean I'm to have that rifle pointed at me the whole way?

THATAWAY JACK. I still got these here diggin's, and until I get them safe at the bank, Pete, you'd best remember that your hat is a useless luxury without a head to park it on.

PEVERAL. That's it! That's it!!! How much do you figure those precious diggin's of yours are worth?

THATAWAY JACK. Oh, about 50 dollars.

PEVERAL. 50 dollars? Okay, now here. *(Pulls out 50 dollars from his pants and hands it to THATAWAY JACK, who lowers the rifle.)* Now give me those two bags of gold. *(THATAWAY does so.)* Now look! *(HE opens the bags and scatters the dust on the ground.)* See? Okay? Any more problems?

THATAWAY JACK. Just one. *(HE raises the rifle and points it at PEVERAL)* Now you know I got 50 dollars *cash,* and *until* them banks open I wouldn't be makin' any sudden movements!

PEVERAL. Tell me, Thataway, are the people in Laramie anything like you?

THATAWAY JACK. *(laughing)* Oh no! They's colorful!

BLACKOUT
END OF SCENE I

SCENE 2

SCENE: The Laramie Inn.

TIME: Three days later.

AT RISE: On stage at present are AMBROSE and ELEANOR
RAVENCROFT, the new proprietors of The Laramie Inn.
They are from back East, having only recently acquired the
property, and are dressed accordingly. At present, AM-
BROSE has just finished putting a banner reading "Grand
Opening" in the window, and steps back to admire his work.
Meanwhile, ELEANOR is busy arranging little vases of
flowers on the tables, which (for this neck of the woods) are
incongruously adorned with lace tablecloths, crocheted place
settings, napkin rings on cloth napkins, and candles. There
is also a chandelier hanging from the ceiling.

ELEANOR. Ambrose, do you know where the silver
cream pitcher is?

AMBROSE. The silver cream pitcher?

ELEANOR. I thought it would a nice touch, if we served
cafe au lait with the dessert.

AMBROSE. Eleanor, darling, this is the Wild West —
not Cleveland.

ELEANOR. *(suddenly distraught)* I know, I know! *(AM-*
BROSE tries to comfort her by gently placing his hands on her
shoulders from behind.) Ahhhh!

AMBROSE. Something the matter, dear?

ELEANOR. I want to go home! Oh Ambrose, this isn't our style. Let's go back to Cleveland. I can't stand it here. The relentless battle for survival. The barroom brawls, the shootouts, the bloodshed, the constant fear of outlaws and Indians. I have nightmares every night! I can't take it anymore! I tell you, I can't take it!

AMBROSE. Darling, we've only been here two days.

ELEANOR. Is that all? *(SHE sobs.)*

AMBROSE. Now Eleanor, try to get a grip on yourself. Uncle Ephraim sold us this place for a song because he knew we were capable of building a life out West ... he knew we were determined to pursue the American Dream ... he knew that we had pioneer blood in our veins!

ELEANOR. He knew that we had nine hundred dollars cash on the barrelhead!

AMBROSE. Alright, but you've got to admit the place is a steal...

ELEANOR. I'm sure the outlaws and the bandits will agree with you.

AMBROSE. ...there's hardly any overhead...

ELEANOR. I've seen the roof.

AMBROSE. Just give it a chance, darling. You've done wonders with this place.

ELEANOR. *(brightening, somewhat)* You really think so?

AMBROSE. Certainly. The Belgian lace, the Limoges china ... They're really quite charming.

ELEANOR. And the chandelier?

AMBROSE. The chandelier? Why ... *(choosing his words carefully)* ...I'll bet everyone who comes in will have something to say about that! *(HE twitches: a sharp movement of his head to one side,* always *accompanied by a decided involuntary wink.)* Oh no.

ELEANOR. I'm sorry, Ambrose. Now look what I've done. I've made you nervous and your twitch is acting up again. I don't mean to be disagreeable.

AMBROSE. *(sympathetically)* I know you don't, dear. *(twitches)*

ELEANOR. I honestly want to make things work.

AMBROSE. I know you do, darling. *(twitches)*

ELEANOR. I'm really trying.

AMBROSE. I know you are, my love. There, I think the twitch is better now. The doctor said getting away from the pressures of city living would help it. *(Embracing her tenderly.)* Now, you mustn't worry. We haven't had any shootouts or outlaws yet, have we?

ELEANOR. No. I suppose not. But Ambrose, I do worry about Indians.

AMBROSE. Nonsense. Indians don't just walk into a place of business in the middle of the day. *(ELEANOR breaths easier.)* Now you finish with the tables, while I go find that creamer for you.

(AMBROSE exits, to the back room. Eleanor goes back to arranging the flowers on the table. TALKING BOAR, an Indian dressed in buckskins and feathers and wearing war-paint, stalks menacingly into the tavern, bearing a tomahawk. HE takes in the situation, then approaches ELEANOR from behind. HE lifts the tomahawk slowly, then lightly taps her on the shoulder. ELEANOR is dumbstruck.)

TALKING BOAR. *(very bright British dialect)* Pardon me,

but you wouldn't by any chance be the proprietor of this establishment? Oh, I say, charming chandelier!

ELEANOR. *(Beat, then screams.)* Ahhhhhhhhhhhhhh! Savages!

TALKING BOAR. *(Looking behind him for savages, screams.)* Ahhhhhhhhhhhhhhhhhhh! *(ELEANOR runs behind the bar and ducks.)*

AMBROSE. *(running in with a rifle)* What is it!

TALKING BOAR. Savages! *(Runs behind the bar and ducks, ELEANOR immediately screams, jumps up and runs behind AMBROSE.)*

ELEANOR. Shoot him, Ambrose! Shoot him!

TALKING BOAR. *(from behind the bar)* Yes, old man. Get the lead out and shoot him! *(AMBROSE slowly walks up to the bar and points the rifle down)*

AMBROSE. I think she means you.

TALKING BOAR. *(Popping his head up from behind the bar.)* Oh. Me?

ELEANOR. Shoot him, Ambrose. He's a savage!

TALKING BOAR. *I'm* a savage? *(Pointing to AMBROSE'S tie.)* Well, at least I know how to tie a knot properly. May I? *(Reaches to adjust AMBROSE'S tie.)*

AMBROSE. *(Slapping his hands away.)* What are you doing here? Is there an Indian uprising?

TALKING BOAR. That's rich! What are you doing here? Are Certified Public Accountants on the rampage?

AMBROSE. I happen to be the owner of this tavern.

TALKING BOAR. Well, ·I happen to be a· potential patron.

AMBROSE. He looks harmless enough, dear.

ELEANOR. *(vehemently)* Knock him out, tie him up, and

lock him in the smokehouse, Ambrose!!

AMBROSE. *(Sticking the rifle in Talking Boar's gut.)* What do you say to that, Injun?

TALKING BOAR. Well, personally, I was hoping for something on the mezzaine level.

AMBROSE. *(Lowering the rifle.)* You know, Darling, he doesn't sound particularly dangerous.

ELEANOR. *(very vehemently)* He's part of an ambush. Hang him upside down by his feet, tape his eyes open and tie his hands with barbed wire!!!

TALKING BOAR. Charming wife you have there.

AMBROSE. Now what do you say, Redskin? *(Pokes him with the rifle again.)*

TALKING BOAR. Do you serve canapes with breakfast?

AMBROSE. My dearest love, I'm sorry but my sixth sense for danger just isn't picking up anything. *(Putting the gun away.)* He's perfectly harmless.

ELEANOR. Amborse, he could steal me in the middle of the night. Take me to his tribe. Would you want to see me live with redskins the rest of my life?

AMBROSE. No dear, of course not, but...

TALKING BOAR. Perhaps I could clear something up. Do you have a reservation for a T. Boar?

AMBROSE. Why, yes we do. *(Picks up the reservation book.)* Even an advance deposit.

TALKING BOAR. That's me. *(Looking at the book.)* T. Boar. Talking Boar. Only it's not spelled B.O.R.E. It's B.O.A.R., like the ferocious animal?

AMBROSE. Excuse my asking, but you don't really sound...

TALKING BOAR. Ah, the accent.

AMBROSE. Are you really an Indian?

TALKING BOAR. Iroquois, actually. You see, my grand-father, Patient Bear, Chief of the Iroquois, befriended the English during the War of 1812. One of their generals, by way of gratitude, later sent me to England for an education. Something to do with bridging the gap between the Indian and the white man. *(with a glance toward ELEANOR)* Optimistic blighter, what? Well anyway, four years at Oxford and a smattering of Tactics at Sandhurst. When I returned, I was full of enthusiasm and ideas. I planned Elizabethan dramas, tea clubs, debating societies and parliamentary procedures. My ideas received a mixed reaction from the tribe. Half of them were in favor of burning me at the stake, while the other half wanted to stake me to an ant hill. Fortunately, my father, the Chief, interceded on my behalf, and I was merely banished from the tribe.

AMBROSE. And now?

TALKING BOAR. Unfortunately, my degree from Oxford was in Norse Literature, a field in which it is difficult to find steady work. So, for the time being, at least, I've secured a position as the Faithful Indian Companion of Fargo Callahan. You have heard of him, I hope?

AMBROSE. No. I can't say I have.

ELEANOR. I've read about him, Ambrose. He's the Rhyming Cowboy.

TALKING BOAR. Really nothing more than a self-appointed upholder of law and order in the West. At any rate, he'll be here soon. He always sends me ahead to do scouting and things of that nature. He has rather romantic ideas of how things ought to be handled.

AMBROSE. We'll be glad to accommodate you in any way we can.

TALKING BOAR. Splendid. Now Fargo is going to come through that front door any second. He's a basically shy, if great, man who is embarrassed by the demonstrations of good will and adoration which greet him wherever he appears. So I hope you will try to keep that to a minimum. Of course you'll want some pictures. *(beat pause)* You do have a photographer in this town? *(They nod.)* Good. He'll no doubt want a full layout for the Sunday supplement and a press release on why Fargo has come to town. Our angle is really to keep it low profile...

(The sound of HORSES HOOVES are heard outside. EVERYONE rushes to the front door, as FARGO CALLAHAN enters through the back door. He is dressed immaculately in white.)

FARGO. I never come where I'm expected, and I'm never expected when I come. That's how I win all my showdowns against vermin and scum.

TALKING BOAR. That's why we never get any press.

AMBROSE. Well it's an honor to have you.

FARGO. Talking Boar, I told you to forget about the press. Remember, we don't fight evil for the glory. We do it to make the West safe for decent folk like these. *(Looking out the window.)* We must be prepared for any eventuality. Talking Boar, I must know if it will rain soon. *(To Ambrose and Eleanor.)* The simple savage mind, unfettered by the white man's knowledge, has developed instincts that far surpass our own.

TALKING BOAR. *(Taking a barometer out of his pouch.)* A drop in the barometric pressure indicates the arrival of a low front which should increase the possibility of precipitation to 80% by nightfall.

FARGO. *(To Eleanor and Ambrose.)* I apologize for that. He's usually very good. *(To TALKING BOAR.)* No, my Red friend. Look out the window and tell me if that grey smoke from the pipe of the Great Northern Spirit means he will weep over the land by evening. Look, and tell us what you see.

TALKING BOAR. Ah yes, wise one. Much sorrow in heart of the Great Northern Spirit.

FARGO. Good, Talking Boar! Go on.

TALKING BOAR. And ... uh ... he's got a mild case of dandruff...

FARGO. Oh ... It may snow. Thank you, my Red Friend. *(He hands some Indian beads to Talking Boar, who smiles wanly and puts them in his pouch. To Ambrose and Eleanor.)* I told you he was good.

AMBROSE. Well, we're very grateful, Mr. Callahan. I hope your trip here is one of rest and relaxation?

FARGO. No, I'm afraid it's business. I'm after the West's most notoriously mean and rotten outlaw.

ELEANOR. Oh my no!

FARGO. Yes. A man so evil he'd sell his mother for a drop of rye whiskey. So foul that full grown panthers hurl themselves off cliffs to avoid him.

TALKING BOAR. Why, he's not even a registered voter, if you can imagine such a thing.

AMBROSE. *(laughing)* Ah, ha ha ha. Well, if you'll just sign the register...

FARGO. Of course. *(Snapping his fingers.)* Talking Boar.

TALKING BOAR. Ahead of you, wise one. *(Crosses to the desk, taking his feather out, dips it in the inkwell and signs the register.)*

FARGO. How much do we owe you?

AMBROSE. Oh, we couldn't charge a celebrity like yourself. I mean what with trying to make the West safe for decent folks.

FARGO. Much obliged.

ELEANOR. I'm going to prepare a special supper for our Grand Opening.

FARGO. A good woman ... a good knife. Both must be sharp, only one can be your wife. Ha ha. *(TALKING BOAR cues AMBROSE & ELEANOR and everyone laughs. Then seriously.)* So, how *is* the crime situation?

AMBROSE. Crime situation?

FARGO. You know, like bank robberies, or corrupt sheriffs, or cattle rustling.

AMBROSE. Oh, nothing like that at all. It's all been quite peaceful actually.

ELEANOR. *(laughing)* Except for the Murphy twins who keep hiding our milking pail.

AMBROSE. *(chuckling)* And they painted our rooster with spots to make it look like it had chicken pox.

FARGO. *(Draws his gun, deadly serious.)* Time I paid the Murphy gang a visit.

ELEANOR. Gang! They're only 10 years old!

FARGO. *(Checking the bullets in his gun.)* Shouldn't be too hard to spot, then.

ELEANOR. Just what do you think you're going to do? They're only children?

FARGO. Don't worry ma'am. I love children. I only mean to scare them a little. Nudge them on the path of law and justice. Cover me from the balcony, Talking Boar. *(Exits out the back.)*

ELEANOR. But they were just having fun! *(SHE hurries out after him. TALKING BOAR bounds up the stairs, with AMBROSE in pursuit.)*

AMBROSE. Hey, what's going on here? We haven't got a balcony.

(THEY exit to one of the rooms. THATAWAY JACK enters the Inn. He goes over to the hotel desk and rings the BELL.)

THATAWAY JACK. Now remember, Pete ... *(Turns around and sees PEVERAL isn't with him.)* Pete! *(Crosses to the doorway.)* Come on in, Pete. Whatya waitin' fer?

(PEVERAL enters. He is dressed in jeans, black boots, maroon shirt, black leather west, and a derby. He also wears a gun.)

PEVERAL. I'm sorry, Thataway, but I don't think this is going to work.

THATAWAY JACK. Pete, sometimes I think you was out settin' fire to an ant hill when the Good Lord give out brains.

PEVERAL. I nearly shot my foot off this morning!

THATAWAY JACK. That's why I filled yer guns with blanks. Honest to God, Pete, talking to you is like trying to make a treaty with a Cigar Store Indian! You want to find Lucy as quick as possible, don't ya?

PEVERAL. Sure.

THATAWAY JACK. Then the way to go about it is to let her find you. That's why you have to pretend to be Derby Dan Turner.

PEVERAL. Yes, but let's be realistic. I'm not goin' to scare anyone.

THATAWAY JACK. Nonsense, Pete. Why if I didn't know who you was I'd jump higher than a frog on a hot skillet. Only, I thought to look meaner you wasn't goin' to shave for a couple of days.

PEVERAL. I haven't.

THATAWAY JACK. Oh. Oh I see it now! *Mean* lookin', Pete. 'Specially that one there in the middle of your chin. Looks like a rattler all coiled and ready to STRIKE! *(PEVERAL jumps back slightly.)*

PEVERAL. You got the old wanted posters of Derby Dan?

THATAWAY JACK. Right here. *(Pulls out a couple of posters from beneath his jacket.)* Took 'em down this morning, and I put up the ones with your picture on it in their place. And I listed every possible crime I could think of. Once the Innkeeper sees this, we'll get a room free for sure! Now, go to it, boy!

PEVERAL. Okay. Okay, I'll do the best I can.

(HE draws himself up, pulls his gun out, strides across to the desk, as AMBROSE, unseen, comes back downstairs. PEVERAL pounds on the desk with his gun.)

PEVERAL. Innkeeper! Innkeeper!

AMBROSE. *(Standing right behind him.)* Yes, sir? *(PEVERAL starts and jumps back.)* May I help you?

PEVERAL. *(Regaining his composure.)* I'm Derby Dan Turner. And I want a room! *(pounds once more)*

AMBROSE. *(going behind the desk)* Certainly, sir. Five dollars ... or six dollars with a bath. And I'm afraid I'll have to ask you for payment in advance.

PEVERAL. Payment? Ain't you never heard of Derby Dan Turner?

AMBROSE. Hmmmmmmmmm......no.

PEVERAL. No! What's the matter? Ya been livin' in a hole all your life?

AMBROSE. Well ... Cleveland. My wife and I just moved out here.

PEVERAL. Well, I guess some identification is in order. My card. *(He takes a large Wanted poster out of his vest and hands it to Ambrose.)*

AMBROSE. *(regarding it)* Very clean shaven. I like that in a young man.

PEVERAL. Never mind that! Read below there about the robbery, murder, cattle rustling, and claim jumpin'...

AMBROSE. *(reading)* Horse stealing, counterfeiting, inciting Indian wars, and jaywalking.

PEVERAL. *(looking at Thataway)* I had a cold that day!

THATAWAY JACK. But he's feelin' better now!

PEVERAL. That's right. *(looking around the hotel)* Say, pardner, have I committed arson yet?

THATAWAY JACK. Why no! That's one you plum overlooked.

PEVERAL. *(Looking at the poster, HE strikes a match.)* Do you think we can fit it in there? Hate to go to all the trouble if the governor can't read about it.

AMBROSE. *(blowing out the match)* Wait a minute! Wait a minute! As part of our promotion for the new hotel we are offering free rooms and accommodations to our new patrons. Let me show you to your room. *(THEY head upstairs.)*

PEVERAL. Why that's mighty neighborly, mighty neighborly. Just for that I ain't gonna plug ya!

AMBROSE. *(Stops on the staircase landing, between Peveral and Thataway.)* Just one thing. My wife is pretty touchy about outlaws. Personally I believe in fair housing, but if you could play down the outlaw bit, I'd be much obliged.

THATAWAY JACK. Reckon we could accomodate ya.

PEVERAL. Reckon. Why don't you just tell her I'm in the banking business. Ha ha ha!

AMBROSE. *(laughing nervously)* Ha ha! Very amusing. Thank you. Shall I show you your room? *(Twitches and winks, in PEVERAL'S direction.)*

PEVERAL. What was that?

AMBROSE. *(turns to Thataway Jack)* Shall I show you your room? *(twitches and winks)*

THATAWAY JACK. Uh ... We'll manage.

(THEY go up to their room, giving a sideways glance at AMBROSE, who twitches once more. THEY hurry into the room. ELEANOR enters.)

ELEANOR. Another customer, dear?

AMBROSE. Yes, darling. A Mr. Turner.

ELEANOR. Not another hero, I hope. We can't afford to

keep giving away our rooms.

AMBROSE. No dear, not another hero.

ELEANOR. Well he's respectable, I hope.

AMBROSE. Very respectable, Darling. In the banking business.

ELEANOR. Did he pay you?

AMBROSE. *(Ringing open the cash register.)* Oh yes, my love. *(Pulls a coin from his vest pocket.)* See? Everything is under control. *(with forced enthusiasm)* This place is a gold mine!

ELEANOR. Ambrose, did you get the groceries for dinner? I'm having trouble finding the ingredients for the Coquilles St. Jacques.

AMBROSE. *(controlling his frustration)* My dear, the General Store didn't have those ingredients. And to save time, I will tell you that I couldn't find ingredients for Cointreau Fruit Delight, or for Chocolate Souffle or for Veal Paprikash a la Roquefort. The General Store had exactly two items. Potatoes and salted beef jerky. They're on the wagon.

ELEANOR. I suppose I'll just have to do something with those. *(exits)*

AMBROSE. I'm sure you'll think of something.

(THATAWAY comes downstairs and is about to say soemthing to Ambrose when an ear-piercing SCREAM is heard. A YOUNG WOMAN, [LUCY] stumbles in, exhausted, with her coat torn.)

LUCY. Indian attack! *(SHE collapses on the floor.)*

AMBROSE. *(Rushes to her, holds her up.)* Indian attack? Where?

LUCY. Five miles north of town. Stage attacked and ... and I hid in some brush and walked all night long.

ELEANOR. *(rushing in)* Did I hear someone say Indian attack!?

AMBROSE. *(Drops Lucy, and goes to Eleanor.)* Now just take it easy, darling ... Nobody said anything about an Indian attack.

THATAWAY JACK. 'Cept this young lady here.

ELEANOR. *(ear piercing)* Ahhhhhhhh! Oh Ambrose, I'm so frightened.

(FARGO enters.)

FARGO. Good news, folks! I found your milk pail!

AMBROSE. Forget about the milkpail! This woman has been attacked!

FARGO. Attacked! Dog-gone those Murphy twins! *(yelling upstairs)* Talking Boar! *(Takes out his gun again.)*

AMBROSE. Not the Murphy twins! Indians!

(TALKING BOAR emerges on the landing in a satin robe with an embroidered crest on one side, and a bath towel wrapped around his head.)

TALKING BOAR. Indians!

FARGO. I'll handle this. *(to LUCY)* Young lady, I must ask you a few questions.

LUCY. I think ... I'm going ... to fa ... to fa ... *(SHE falls in a heap.)*

FARGO. Ah, if only we knew what she was trying to say? *(slowly)* I think I'm going to...

AMBROSE. *(helping him)* I think I'm going to *faint!*

FARGO. Good Lord, not you, too. I've got enough on my hands already.

ELEANOR. No, that's what the *girl* was saying! Look, There's an arrow stuck in her purse.

FARGO. Hmmm ... What kind of arrow is this, Talking Boar?

TALKING BOAR. *(scanning it)* Hmmmm ... uh, oh.

FARGO. What is it?

TALKING BOAR. It's an Indian arrow!

ELEANOR. *(Grabbing the arrow from TALKING BOAR.)* Ambrose, help me get this poor girl upstairs. *(THEY help LUCY up and take her up to one of the rooms.)* Now where did she say those Indians were?

AMBROSE. Don't worry, Eleanor. They're five miles north of town.

FARGO. If I could only discover where they are ... Talking Boar, do you think together we could track them?

TALKING BOAR. Possible, but it depends.

FARGO. On what?

TALKING BOAR. On how far you can carry me screaming and kicking.

FARGO. Say, Talking Boar, you're not nervous are you?

TALKING BOAR. Nervous?! Listen, my good man, not all Indians come out of Oxford. Some of them come from Cambridge! I wouldn't stand a chance. Besides, I'm hardly dressed for it.

FARGO. Very well, I'll go alone. Now, she said "five miles north of town." That's ... uh ... *(trying to figure out where north is)* ...no, let's see...

THATAWAY JACK. *(pointing)* It's thataway. But I wouldn't worry 'bout findin' them. They'll find you.

FARGO. Are you suggesting my outfit may be too conspicuous?

THATAWAY JACK. I'm saying this is gonna be Sitting Bull meets Sitting Duck. Why don't you just take some sequins and sew a bulls-eye on your back?

FARGO. *(impressed)* Say, you seem to know something about this.

(TOM TOM'S come in low and build.)

THATAWAY JACK. Never mind, Buffalo Bill, looks like they found us.

(PEVERAL emerges on the landing.)

PEVERAL. What's going on, Thataway?

THATAWAY JACK. Indian attack, looks like.

PEVERAL. Oh. What!!!?

(HE heads downstairs, as AMBROSE emerges from another room carrying a rifle, and heads downstairs as well.)

THATAWAY JACK. Everybody better take some cover, and if you got a gun, use it. *(EVERYBODY grabs some cover. AMBROSE by the window. PEVERAL takes up station next to THATAWAY.)*

PEVERAL. What will they do if they capture us?

THATAWAY JACK. Way I figure it, they'll probably torture us ... and scalp us.

PEVERAL. Torture and scalp us?

THATAWAY JACK. Could be worse, you know. Could be worse.

PEVERAL. What could be worse than scalping?!

THATAWAY JACK. They could have them a *dull* tomahawk.

(DRUMS get louder.)

PEVERAL. Why do they have to beat that drum so loud?

THATAWAY JACK. That's so's you'll know they're up to something.

FARGO. What are they up to?

THATAWAY JACK. Beatin' that drum, I guess.

TALKING BOAR. It's giving me a splitting headache.

THATAWAY JACK. I don't think you want their headache cure. Besides, you don't have to worry 'till them drums *stop*.

(The DRUMS STOP beating.)

PEVERAL. It's quiet. What does that mean?

THATAWAY JACK. Means they've done had their fill of beatin' that drum.

(There is a tense pause, during which all eyes are trained on the front entrance. A door opens upstairs and everyone quickly turns and trains a gun on Eleanor as she steps out on the landing.)

ELEANOR. Don't shoot!

AMBROSE. Eleanor, get down. The Indians are attacking!

(The DRUMS start up again.)

AMBROSE. Hear that?

ELEANOR. *(Quite calmly, coming downstairs.)* Ambrose, look out the window. *(AMBROSE slowly and cautiously gets up and looks out the window. All eyes go with him.)*

AMBROSE. Well I'll be. It's those Murphy Twins!

FARGO. *(beat)* The Murphy gang again! Talking Boar, cover me from the balcony! *(FARGO rushes out.)*

ELEANOR. *(Following FARGO with AMBROSE.)* Now wait a minute. They're just playing a game! *(TALKING BOAR yawns and goes upstairs.)*

THATAWAY JACK. *(Looks out the window.)* Why they couldn't be more'n ten years old. *(looks at PEVERAL)* Say Pete, you look more pale than a cotton ball in a bucket of whitewash. You better go up and rest a while.

PEVERAL. *(A little shakey, and still holding his gun tightly with both hands.)* It was just the Murphy twins. No Indians.

THATAWAY JACK. *(Leading him upstairs.)* That's right Pete. Just the Murphy twins. Now why don't you let go of that gun? It's just got blanks in it. All you can give anybody is an earache.

PEVERAL. Just ten year old boys?

THATAWAY JACK. Yeah ... But they's big for their age, Pete! Real big!

(THEY exit. AMBROSE & ELEANOR enter.)

AMBROSE. Will you please tell me what's going on? What about that girl?

ELEANOR. She just told me she made up the whole story so we'd feel sorry for her and take her in. She's asleep now. She was practically dead of exhaustion and hunger.

AMBROSE. Well that's a hell of a way to meet people.

ELEANOR. I'm sure she was quite desperate, Ambrose. Now help me light the stove. It's been acting up. Afterall, we've still got a hotel to run.

AMBROSE. Yeah, and I'm not exactly crazy about the clientele we've been attracting. *(twitches)* Why can't we get someone nice a quiet for a change? *(THEY exit.)*

(DERBY DAN TURNER appears at the swinging doors of the entrance. HE is dressed mostly in black, wears one black glove and wears a derby as well. HE also sports a single black holster and six-gun, which he wears strapped directly in front of his groin. HE shoves the doors open, then steps inside, looking around. OFFSTAGE, the TOM TOMS are heard again. DERBY slowly wheels, unholsters his gun and FIRES out into the street. There is silence for a beat, then the sound of the TOM TOMS dropping on the ground. DERBY puts the gun slowly back into his holster, holding onto it for a moment, in obvious ecstasy. HE goes to a table and puts some silverware into his saddlebag, then blows his nose on a napkin and throws it back onto the plate. HE heads over to the counter. When he speaks it is with a decided Irish accent. He is one moment very light on the surface, and the next moment exploding, or laughing maniacally.)

DERBY DAN. Innkeeper? Innkeeper? *(Strolls over to the*

chandelier and regards it.) INNKEEPER!

(ELEANOR enters.)

ELEANOR. Yes, sir?

DERBY DAN. Where did this come from?! *(Moves to where Eleanor is standing, looking her up and down.)*

ELEANOR. It's imported from London. Do you like it?

DERBY DAN. *(still regarding ELEANOR)* It's a nice piece of work.

ELEANOR. What can I do for you, Mister...?

DERBY DAN. My name is Turner... Derby Dan Turner! That name mean anything to ya?

ELEANOR. Turner ... Turner ... oh yes, of course Mr. Turner. My husband told me something about you.

DERBY DAN. Your husband knows a great deal, does he?

ELEANOR. Well, he mentioned you were in the banking business.

DERBY DAN. I guess you could say banks provide me a livin' of sorts.

ELEANOR. Which bank? Maybe we'll make a deposit there.

DERBY DAN. Well the last one I was in could use a deposit.

ELEANOR. Are you staying long?

DERBY DAN. Just passin' through. *(Putting his hand to his neck.)* I don't like to get "hung up" in one place. *(Laughs at his joke.)* And now, about my room...

ELEANOR. How do you like it?

DERBY DAN. Like what?

ELEANOR. Your room.

DERBY DAN. Darlin', that would be difficult to say as I haven't seen it, yet!

ELEANOR. Oh, didn't you get a key?

DERBY DAN. No I haven't got a key! Now listen here...

ELEANOR. *(Looking at the register.)* Well, that's odd. It says here you're all checked in.

DERBY DAN. Checked in, you say? May I see that register?

ELEANOR. Certainly. *(Hands it to him.)*

DERBY DAN. *(HE looks over the register.)* Well, I'll be...

ELEANOR. Something wrong.

DERBY DAN. Uh ... no. I seem to recall leaving the key with your husband.

ELEANOR. I'll go and get him. *(starts to leave)*

DERBY DAN. Wait a minute! *(SHE turns.)* Fargo Callahan?

ELEANOR. Yes, do you know him?

DERBY DAN. I know *of* him. *(with vehement revulsion)* I've heard he dresses in all white, and rhymes his words!

ELEANOR. That's him. He's here to catch the West's most notoriously mean and rotten outlaw. Can you imagine? I'll get my husband. *(SHE exits.)*

DERBY DAN. *(to himself)* Aye, imagine that. Fargo Callahan's in town, and I'm already registered at the hotel. *(Takes out his gun and checks the chamber.)* This should be a very interesting visit.

(AMBROSE enters.)

AMBROSE. Well, Mr. Turner, my wife tells me ... *(Sees DERBY DAN.)* Oh, I'm sorry. I thought Mr. Turner was here. Must have found his key. So, may I be of assistance to you, sir? *(twitches)*

DERBY DAN. *(Grabs Ambrose by the collar.)* How would you be meaning that?

AMBROSE. I only mean what can I, as the owner of this Inn, do for you?

DERBY DAN. *(Pulling him by the collar up onto the counter.)* Tell me this: What the devil is goin' on around here?!

AMBROSE. I thought perhaps you'd like a room.

DERBY DAN. You mentioned a Mr. Turner. Are you speaking of Derby Dan Turner?

AMBROSE. Yes.

DERBY DAN. And you'd recognize this Turner if you saw him?

AMBROSE. Of course. I've seen the Wanted poster.

DERBY DAN. You have? *(Drops him and draws his gun, putting it in his nose.)* Where?

AMBROSE. *(Takes out the Wanted poster and holds it out for Derby.)* Here, have a look for yourself. *(Hands him PEVERAL'S Wanted poster.)*

DERBY DAN. *(Looking at the poster.)* What the devil ... I mean ... so this is the famous Mr. Derby Dan Turner? *(smiling)* I hear he's a pretty nasty fella.

AMBROSE. Yeah, well let's not scare the wife, if you don't mind.

DERBY DAN. I'd like a room if you please.

AMBROSE. Very well. May I suggest our deluxe package weekend, which includes three days and two nights with a bath included, feather pillow, and the ultimate in privacy — no view. *(DERBY DAN spits on the floor.)* Then again, maybe you'd just like a room for the night. *(DERBY DAN nods.)* Fine, under what name?

DERBY DAN. Uh ... Smith.

AMBROSE. *(writing)* Smith ... and the first name?

DERBY DAN. Mister. Now be quick about it!

AMBROSE. Alright, Mr. Smith ... if you'd just sign the register, that'll be five dollars, in advance.

DERBY DAN. *(Having signed the register.)* I'd be much obliged if you'd put it on me bill.

AMBROSE. I'll need some collateral.

DERBY DAN. *(outraged)* What's that!!?

AMBROSE. *(explaining)* That's where I let you have a room on credit, and in return you let me keep something of value.

DERBY DAN. *(Pulling out his gun.)* Now tell me this: Would yer life be value enough for collateral?

AMBROSE. I suppose, if you want to put a literal interpretation on things ... *(DERBY DAN cocks the gun.)* ... makes perfect sense. Your key. *(Hands it over.)*

DERBY DAN. I'm very much beholden to you. And don't trouble yourself showing me up. I'll find it myself. *(HE goes upstairs and exits into one of the rooms.)*

AMBROSE. *(Takes another gold piece out of his pocket.)* If business gets any better, I'll be broke before the end of the day.

(ELEANOR enters.)

ELEANOR. Did you take care of Mr. Turner?

AMBROSE. He must have found his key, dear. We have

another customer now. A Mr. Smith. *(ELEANOR notices the napkin DERBY DAN blew his nose on, and straightens it back up onto the plate.)*

ELEANOR. Did he pay you?

AMBROSE. Oh ... yes ... certainly he did. Look at this! Yessiree, this is a real money making proposition!

ELEANOR. Well, I'm beginning to feel a little better now that some money is coming in. Now I have to go make up tonight's menu.

(ELEANOR exits. AMBROSE twitches, and picks up a bottle of whiskey and takes a slug. LUCY comes downstairs, still dressed in her tattered overcoat.)

AMBROSE. Oh, it's you! Don't you know there are better ways to meet people than by staging phony Indian attacks? *(take a swig)*

LUCY. I'm very sorry about that. But I was tired and hungry and I guess I just lost my head.

AMBROSE. Shhh! Don't ever say "lost my head" in Shawnee country. *(takes a swig)*

LUCY. My name is Lucy and I'm looking for work.

AMBROSE. *(Approaches her, introducing himself.)* Ambrose Ravencroft. Looking for work, huh? What kind of work are you looking for? *(twitches)*

LUCY. *(Slaps him, sending him reeling.)* Certainly not that kind of work!

AMBROSE. *(recovers)* Hold on a second. All I said was what are you interested in? *(twitches)*

LUCY. *(Slugging him in the stomach.)* Not what you've got in mind, you filthy scum!

AMBROSE. *(Trying to regain his breath.)* Hey wait a minute! Just let me explain. You see, I've got this *thing* ... and it acts up whenever I get excited ... *(twitches)* Uh oh. *(LUCY kicks his legs out from under him and he falls on his seat.)* I'm just going to sit here awhile.

(ELEANOR enters.)

ELEANOR. Ambrose! What's happened? *(AMBROSE points at LUCY.)* Did you do this?

LUCY. I certainly did. What's it to you?

ELEANOR. That's my husband.

LUCY. Well, if I were you, ma'am, I'd keep him locked up.

AMBROSE. Somebody lock me up, please. *(twitches)*

ELEANOR. Now his nervous twitch is acting up again.

LUCY. *(embarrassed)* Nervous twitch? Oh. I didn't realize. I'm terribly sorry for all the trouble I've caused. I'll gladly pay you back with hard work. I need a job desperately. I can sing, and dance, and play the piano a bit.

ELEANOR. We could use someone to clean the rooms and sweep out the place.

LUCY. Well ... I suppose I can't be too choosy. I haven't eaten anything for three days...

ELEANOR. I'll fix you a plate of dinner. *(exits)*

AMBROSE. *(getting up)* You haven't eaten for three days?

LUCY. Well nothing but potatoes and beef jerky.

AMBROSE. Bon appetit. Then you'll take the job?

LUCY. Yes, of course. But, I was looking for a job on

the stage, and I'm afraid the only outfit I have is the one I'm wearing. *(SHE takes off her coat, and is wearing a dance hall outfit.)*

AMBROSE. *(swallows, hoarsely)* Just what Eleanor wears when she cleans the rooms. That'll be just fine. But you better be careful, Miss Lucy. There are a lot of crazy people in this town. *(twitch)*

LUCY. Don't worry about me, Mr. Ravencroft...

AMBROSE. Call me Ambrose.

LUCY. Ambrose. I've read all about it ... *(She swings her leg up on a chair, hikes up her skirt, and pulls a derringer out from her garter.)* ...and I've come prepared.

AMBROSE. Call me Mr. Ravencroft. Beautiful gun you got there.

LUCY. It's a pearl-handled derringer left me by my papa. *(AMBROSE looks at it as SHE puts it away.)*

(ELEANOR enters from behind him.)

LUCY. I believe a girl should be prepared for anything. *(AMBROSE is looking at the gun in her garter.)*

AMBROSE. What a beauty. I don't know when I've seen a finer piece. *(ELEANOR slams a bottle down on the bar, AMBROSE turns around and see ELEANOR scowling at him.)*

LUCY. I was just showing Mr. Ravencroft my derringer. *(Takes her leg down.)* I can't thank you enough for the job. I've only just arrived out here and I don't know what I'd do if it weren't for your kindness.

ELEANOR. Well ... have yourself something to eat. *(Gives her a plate of jerky and potatoes. LUCY starts upstairs.)*

You can get some rest and start in the morning. Take number four upstairs. I think Ambrose has seen quite enough for one day, right, Ambrose?

AMBROSE. Yes, my love. *(twitches)*

LUCY. Thanks again. *(Exits into her room.)*

ELEANOR. Care to have a look at the menu? *(Shows him the menu, which he takes and opens and reads.)*

AMBROSE. Potatoes ... Beef Jerky ... no surprises so far ... Potatoes stuffed with Beef Jerky ... Mashed potatoes with Diced Beef Jerky ... puréed Jerky and Potatoes.

ELEANOR. That's the special.

(PEVERAL and THATAWAY enter and head downstairs.)

AMBROSE. Absolutely mouth-watering, dear. Keep and eye on the desk. I'll check the stove.

PEVERAL. *(in normal voice)* I wonder if I might have a menu.

(TALKING BOAR enters and heads for one of the tables.)

ELEANOR. Certainly. *(Hands him one.)* Here you are.

PEVERAL. *(Glancing over it.)* Hmm. *(THATAWAY nudges PEVERAL, reminding him to stay in character.)* Don't you got anythin' more substantial? I've eaten better food in prison.

ELEANOR. Oh my! You've been in prison?

PEVERAL. Yeah ... four years in ... uh ... Fairhaven.

TALKING BOAR. *(Taking a seat, from across the room.)* What a coincidence! I was at Fairhaven for a year. In fact I transferred because they couldn't serve a decent meal.

PEVERAL. *(to Eleanor)* Poor savage. I guess they beat him so senseless he withdrew into a world of his own making.

TALKING BOAR. You weren't on the rowing team by any chance?

PEVERAL. See what I mean?

THATAWAY JACK. You'll excuse us while we take this bottle to that poor soul and do him a kindness. *(THEY cross to Talking Boar's table. ELEANOR exits.)*

PEVERAL. Say, who are you?

THATAWAY JACK. You claiming to be an Injun?

TALKING BOAR. Iroquois.

THATAWAY JACK. But you palaver in the white man's tongue good as me.

TALKING BOAR. I would hope that my grasp of the English language is at least syntactically correct, if somewhat less colorful than your own. I'm also fluent in the French, German and Norwegian languages, and can read Greek and Latin a bit. As a matter of fact I translated Ibsen's *Hedda Gabler* into English for my Master's thesis project. Nonetheless, I thank you for the compliment.

PEVERAL. What's your name?

TALKING BOAR. My name is Boar. Talking Boar.

THATAWAY JACK. It figures. Boy you got more jaw than a two-headed crocodile. When your tongue gets to flapping it could beat a spike into a railroad tie. I guess it ain't too hard to figure out why you was banished from the tribe.

TALKING BOAR. Who said I was banished from the tribe?

THATAWAY JACK. The Iroquois nation is over two thousand miles away. Your horse couldn't throw you this far, though I couldn't blame it for trying. What you doing so far from home?

TALKING BOAR. I'm afraid your instincts aren't entirely off base. I was banished from the tribe. In fact, my fiancee, Bouncing Feathers, was the one who led the movement. So now I am gainfully employed as the faithful Indian friend of Fargo Callahan.

THATAWAY JACK. Fargo Callahan?! Is that who your friend is? *(TALKING BOAR nods.)*

PEVERAL. Fargo Callahan? Who's he?

TALKING BOAR. He's the Rhyming Cowboy — the man who's out to get Derby Dan Turner alive or dead. *(PEVERAL and THATAWAY look at each other.)* Whom do I have the pleasure of addressing?

PEVERAL. Me? *(Quickly takes off the derby he's wearing.)*

(ELEANOR enters.)

PEVERAL. I'm ... uh ... Mr. Smith.

THATAWAY JACK. Thataway Jack's the name.

TALKING BOAR. Pleasure to meet you, Smith. You too, Jack. Now if you'll excuse me, I must report to Fargo. Cheerio! *(exits upstairs)*

ELEANOR. Have you decided on anything to eat yet, Mr. Smith?

PEVERAL. No. No, we'll be checking out right now. Gotta run and get my things. Excuse me. *(PEVERAL & THATAWAY run upstairs into their room.)*

ELEANOR. But I've just prepared a beek jerky gravy.

(As THEY slam the door shut, DERBY DAN'S opens and HE steps out on the landing.)

DERBY DAN. I wonder if you'd mind sending up a newspaper. I want to check the financial reports. You can bring it yourself, darlin'. *(HE puts his hand on his gun.)* And if Danny's a bad boy, you might even give him a spankin'! *(DERBY goes slowly back to his room singing "Danny Boy.")*

ELEANOR. *(completely in shock)* Certainly.

(AMBROSE enters from the back room.)

AMBROSE. I think I've got the stove fixed, dear.

ELEANOR. *(still in shock)* Mr. Smith wants to check out, I'm afraid. Will you tabulate his bill? And Mr. Turner would like a newspaper to check the financial pages. Here's a plate of beef jerky for you.

AMBROSE. Thank you, dear. *(ELEANOR exits.)*

(FARGO comes out on the landing.)

FARGO. I heard footsteps. Everything alright down there?

AMBROSE. Fine. Just fine! *(twitches)*

FARGO. *(coming downstairs)* I see. Nobody is forcing you to say that?

AMBROSE. Of course not. *(twitches)*

FARGO. *(Winking back at him.)* Sure, sure I understand. *(Slowly looks all around the Inn.)* Is that a closet?

AMBROSE. Yes, but each room has its own. You needn't use that one. *(twitches)*

FARGO. *(Winking back at him.)* Farthest thing from my mind.

(FARGO flings open the closet door and shoots into it several times.)

AMBROSE. What are you doing! *(Pulls his coat from the closet, and it's filled with holes.)* Why'd you do that? There's nobody here!

FARGO. Must have slipped past me. I'll check outside.

(HE exits out the back just as the door opens and THATAWAY JACK starts down the stairs.)

THATAWAY JACK. Got any beef jerky?

AMBROSE. My wife will be serving dinner, shortly.

THATAWAY JACK. I need it for the road. Ain't you heard we're leavin'? Now where's the beef jerky?

AMBROSE. Well it's mighty rare in these parts. *(Takes the piece off his plate.)* Ah, here's some. And here's the newspaper.

THATAWAY JACK. What fer?

AMBROSE. My wife said Mr. Turner wants to check the financial pages. *(Hands the paper to Thataway.)*

THATAWAY JACK. *(Shaking his head, as HE goes back upstairs.)* Sounds just like him. He never wants to waste his time robbing banks that ain't financially sound. *(THATAWAY exits.)*

AMBROSE. *(Calling after him.)* I'll saddle your horses presently. *(to himself)* Deadbeats!

(FARGO enters from behind through the back door.)

FARGO. Everything okay?

AMBROSE. *(jumping, startled)* Ahhhh! Oh, it's you again!

FARGO. Our friend must have eluded me, eh? *(winks)*

AMBROSE. You ruined my coat. I told you there's nobody here. Are you bananas? *(twitches)*

FARGO. *(winking)* Bananas ... of course. We keep *bananas* in the *kitchen,* don't we?

(He flings open the kitchen curtains and fires inside several times.)

AMBROSE. *(Rushing into the kitchen.)* What are you doing? *(Comes out with a copper kettle full of holes.)*

FARGO. *(looking inside)* He must have slipped out the window. Tell Talking Boar to cover the back. *(Exits through the kitchen.)*

AMBROSE. Why don't we just call the cavalry in?

(AMBROSE sees DERBY DAN.)

AMBROSE. Ah, Mr. Smith, so sorry you'll be leaving us, but I'm still going to have to charge you for half a day.

DERBY DAN. What would be giving you the impression I'm leavin', worm! I've no intention of goin' anywhere! *(Starts to pull out his gun.)*

AMBROSE. That's wonderful.

DERBY DAN. Now would you be so kind as to send a

paper up to me room? *(AMBROSE twitches.)* And stop winking at me!

(DERBY DAN exits. as LUCY comes out of her room bearing her empty plate.)

AMBROSE. Hadn't you better rest up, young lady?
LUCY. Oh I feel better now that I've had something to eat. *(SHE trips and falls into Ambrose's arms.)* Oh, I'm terribly sorry!
AMBROSE. No trouble at all.

(ELEANOR enters.)

AMBROSE. She tripped.
LUCY. I tripped.
ELEANOR. *(an iceberg)* Oh, I see.
LUCY. Perhaps I'd better go rinse my plate. *(exits)*
ELEANOR. Perhaps *you'd* better go saddle up Mr. Smith's horse, dear. Has he checked out yet?
AMBROSE. Dearest, he seems to have had a change of heart. *He's* staying, but *Mr. Turner* wants to leave. I'll go attend to it. Oh and *Mr. Smith* wants a copy of the paper, now.

(AMBROSE exits. LUCY enters from back room.)

ELEANOR. Oh Lucy, would you mind taking this paper up and putting it outside Mr. Smith's door.
LUCY. Certainly. *(Takes the paper and heads upstairs.)*
ELEANOR. I believe I saw him going into room three.
(LUCY drops the paper outside Peveral's door.)

ELEANOR. Oh, and Lucy. *(LUCY turns to her.)* Watch your step, dear.

LUCY. Yes, ma'am.

(SHE exits into her room, as PEVERAL enters and trips over the newspaper, picks it up and comes downstairs.)

ELEANOR. Ah, Mr. Smith. So glad you've decided to stay with us.

PEVERAL. Now get this straight. I'm leaving. I need my horse saddled, I need my canteen filled, and I don't need any more newspapers. *(Tosses it in the back room.)*

ELEANOR. Very well, Mr. Smith. I'll be back in a jiffy.

(ELEANOR exits to the kitchen. PEVERAL standing with his back to the staircase, as DERBY DAN comes down the steps.)

DERBY DAN. Where the devil can a man get a newspaper around here!

PEVERAL. *(back to him)* Try the back room.

DERBY DAN. Much obliged, stranger.

PEVERAL. Forget it.

DERBY DAN. Lousy service.

PEVERAL. You can say that again. *(DERBY DAN exits to the back room. ELEANOR enters with the canteen filled.)*

ELEANOR. Here you are, Mr. Smith.

PEVERAL. Thanks. Now please send someone up for my saddlebags.

(HE exits to his room, as AMBROSE enters from the front door.)

AMBROSE. Mr. Turner's horse is saddled. Did he check out yet?

ELEANOR. I haven't seen him, dear. But Mr. Smith has changed his mind again. He wants to leave after all.

AMBROSE. Are you sure?

ELEANOR. Yes, he asked that you go get his saddle bags and bring them down.

AMBROSE. You're certain, Eleanor?

ELEANOR. He seemed most impatient about it.

AMBROSE. That sounds like him, alright. *(Goes upstairs, as ELEANOR exits to the back.)* First he's going, then he's not going, then he's going again. *(Opens Derby Dan's door and brings out the saddle bags.)* What next?

(DERBY DAN enters from the back room with newspaper, stops short upon seeing AMBROSE emerge from his room carrying his saddlebags.)

AMBROSE. Well, Mr. Smith, My wife tells me you're leaving after all. We're getting your horse ready and personally, I'm not sorry at all to see you leave.

DERBY DAN. Good! 'Cause I told you I ain't goin'! *(Slugs Ambrose in the stomach, takes the saddle bags and kicks his feet out from under him.)* And if you've nothin' better to do than steal people's saddlebags ... *(Pulls his gun and SHOOTS at the ceiling.)* ... patch the place up a bit!

(DERBY DAN exits into his room, while TALKING BOAR emerges on the landing, smoking a pipe and carrying a snifter of brandy.)

TALKING BOAR. I say, down there. Anyone seen Fargo Callahan?

AMBROSE. He's outside. He wants you to cover the back.

TALKING BOAR. *(coming downstairs)* Cover the back of what?

AMBROSE. How should I know? But if you see him, give him a sedative. *(AMBROSE holds the back door open for Talking Boar.)*

TALKING BOAR. Thanks old chap.

(TALKING BOAR exits back door. FARGO appears through the front door.)

FARGO. Everything okay?

AMBROSE. *(jumping up)* Ahhhh! You again! Did you see what you did to this pot? These things don't grow on trees, you know! *(twitches)*

FARGO. *(winking back)* Of course, you *grow* things in the garden!

AMBROSE. Oh no.

FARGO. Be right back. *(exits out back)*

AMBROSE. What are you doing? I've only got my cow and chickens out back.

(There is a barrage of GUNFIRE.)

AMBROSE. On the bright side, maybe they'll kill each other. *(FARGO enters followed by TALKING BOAR, feather broken in half, holding the remains of the brandy snifter.)*

AMBROSE. No such luck.

FARGO. Looks like he got away this time. *(THEY start upstairs.)* Oh if you don't serve fresh milk or eggs for breakfast tomorrow, no need to apologize. We aren't fussy eaters.

(THEY enter their room and shut the door. AMBROSE twitches three times in a row, takes a bottle of whiskey and takes a swig. LUCY enters from her room struggling with the clasp on her dress.)

AMBROSE. Watch your step, young lady.

LUCY. Oh I will. I was just trying to change into some clothes your wife left with me, but I can't get this clasp undone. Could you help me?

AMBROSE. Certainly. It probably just got bent a little ... *(Starts to undo the clasp, thinks better of it.)* Could you imagine what my wife would think if she saw this? You'd better get her to do it.

LUCY. Perhaps you're right.

(LUCY starts for the back room, and a section of her dress tears off in AMBROSE'S hand, as ELEANOR enters.)

LUCY. Uh ... Mr. Ravencroft was helping me off with my dress.

ELEANOR. Oh?

AMBROSE. *(urgently)* She means ... my hand got caught in her dress!

ELEANOR. Apparently.

AMBROSE. I mean ... she needed help with her clasp. I was sending her in to you, and...

ELEANOR. Perhaps we'll talk later, Ambrose. *(Begins to cry as she exits.)*

AMBROSE. *(to Lucy)* Now look what you've done. *(PEVERAL steps out on the landing.)*

PEVERAL. Is my horse saddled yet?

AMBROSE. Yes, Mr. Turner!

LUCY. *(Looks wide-eyed at Peveral.)* Turner!

AMBROSE. Your horse is saddled! And I would be very happy to cup my hands and give you a boost if you would only get on him and ride away!

PEVERAL. Why hasn't anyone brought down my saddle bags!

AMBROSE. *(Running upstairs to Peveral's room.)* Anything you say, Mr. Turner! Anything you want to get you on your way!

PEVERAL. Thataway, let's go. *(HE and THATAWAY head down the stairs.)*

LUCY. *(Looking at Peveral with big brown eyes.)* Excuse me. Mr. Derby Dan Turner?

THATAWAY JACK. He's not around, miss. *(to Peveral)* Let's go.

PEVERAL. *(Recognizing her instantly, stares at her a moment.)* I'm Derby Dan Turner.

THATAWAY JACK. Why, I didn't see him for a second there! *(to himself)* You done it now, boy. You done it now.

(AMBROSE comes downstairs with his saddle bags.)

AMBROSE. Your saddle bags, Mr. Turner!

PEVERAL. Take 'em back upstairs.

AMBROSE. What!?!?

PEVERAL. Can't you hear, pardner! I said, take 'em back upstairs. I ain't goin' anywhere! Got that! *(AMBROSE starts to lug the saddlebags back upstairs.)*

THATAWAY JACK. Hold on with those a minute. *(AMBROSE starts back down.)* Now Pete — I mean, Derby Dan, let's talk this over. *(THATAWAY pulls Peveral aside.)*

PEVERAL. Thataway, that's Lucy! I have to see her. It's what we came here for. Just give me a little time.

THATAWAY JACK. Okay, but make it quick. Things is heating up. *(to Ambrose)* Here, give me those bags. And Mr. Turner wants the room cleared!

AMBROSE. With pleasure! *(THEY both exit to the back room. PEVERAL and LUCY move toward one of the tables.)*

LUCY. So, you're Derby Dan Turner. I must say, Mr. Turner you're much different from what I was expecting. I don't really know what I was expecting, of course. I ... what I mean is ... you look gentler. Of course your clothing is filthy, and you have the disgusting odor of tobacco about you ... it's quite exciting, in a way. You're a bit shorter than I imagined, but then I guess that's the way it is with legends, would't you say so? *(PEVERAL shrugs.)* My, you're not very talkative are you? Just as I thought. A man of few words who lets his deeds do the talking. *(PEVERAL spits.)* So, you're Derby Dan Turner.

PEVERAL. And you're Lucy.

LUCY. How'd you know my name?

PEVERAL. How did I know your name? *(HE takes her picture out of his wallet and shows it to her.)*

LUCY. Why, that's the picture I mailed to ... Peveral Biddingwell. How did you get this picture?

PEVERAL. Does it matter?

LUCY. Don't tell me you've harmed Peveral?

PEVERAL. Does it matter?

LUCY. You mean he's dead?

PEVERAL. Does it matter?

LUCY. You really are a man of few words. But how? Why? *(PEVERAL is about to speak.)* It doesn't matter, I suppose. *(Takes out a handkerchief and wipes her eyes.)* He was such a nice man. *(sighs)*

PEVERAL. What's he to you?

LUCY. It's a long story. I was to be his mail order bride. I've never even met him.

PEVERAL. *(pause)* That's a long story?

LUCY. He was a banker. I thought that life was what I wanted. And I meant everything I told him, when I said it. But then I started thinking about it...

PEVERAL. And...

LUCY. Well ... how could I ever be content being the wife of a banker after I read this account about you. *(Shows him a book.)*

PEVERAL. *(reading)* "The Wells Fargo Bank That Was Robbed by Derby Dan." Does it tell you all the people I killed?

LUCY. Why, no.

PEVERAL. It oughta. I killed nearly everyone.

LUCY. Who?

PEVERAL. Who? Why ... there was ... well, who you want to know about?

LUCY. The Carnation Kid?

PEVERAL. I planted him!

LUCY. Silver Gun Sam?

PEVERAL. Polished him off!

LUCY. The Farmer Brothers?

PEVERAL. I ploughed 'em under.

LUCY. Wow. I didn't realize...

PEVERAL. Ain't you gonna ask me about the Hole in the Wall Gang?

LUCY. What about the Hole in the Wall Gang?

PEVERAL. I plastered 'em! So you see, maybe life with this Peveral fella wouldn't have been so bad after all.

LUCY. The West is so raw and wild this side of the Pecos! Nothing can match it!

PEVERAL. By gosh, I never quite looked at it that way. But you're right. Bankers lead a pretty boring life, alright. All those years at Fairhaven were a waste.

LUCY. Fairhaven?

PEVERAL. Yeah, Fairhaven. The foulest penitentiary this side ... say, what side of the Pecos *are* we on? Well, it doesn't matter. Every side I'm on is the wrong side!

(DERBY DAN TURNER emerges from his room and heads downstairs. PEVERAL see Derby Dan, gets up.)

PEVERAL. And nobody better forget it! *(Addresses DERBY DAN.)* That your mangy critter tied up outside?

DERBY DAN. Aye, it is. *(THEY slowly cross toward one another until they are nose to nose.)*

PEVERAL. That's *my* hitchin spot! On your way out just leave the saddle, bedroll, rifle and lariat. Call it rent and say I'm in a good mood.

DERBY DAN. And who is it I should say thank you to for

being so understanding?

PEVERAL. Better have a drink first to steady your nerves. I'm Derby Dan Turner!

DERBY DAN. *(smiling)* I do believe I'll have that drink now. *(Pours himself a drink, and begins shuffling a deck of cards.)*

PEVERAL. Sure, go ahead. I understand. Quite a shock, huh? I mean, you realizing you were seconds from dying a horrible death. Well, pull yourself together, PULL YOURSELF TOGETHER, I ain't gonna kill you. Not until I get another gun. Ain't no more room for another notch on the handle of the one I got now.

DERBY DAN. Mighty impressive. Heard you even got Palomino Pete.

PEVERAL. Yeah. I planted that varmint in '68.

DERBY DAN. Odd. I heard he was planted in '66.

PEVERAL. Oh. Well ... yeah ... that's right, but I dug him up and *re*planted him! When I got a score to settle, I settle it. Comprende?

DERBY DAN. Would you care to play a hand or two?

PEVERAL. Don't mind if I do. Don't mind if I do. A hand of what?

DERBY DAN. Poker.

PEVERAL. Poker, of course! One of my favorites! Right up there with blackjack. I learned blackjack from my folks. Rough childhood ... they kept *hitting* me until I was twenty-one.

DERBY DAN. How do you feel about playing for big stakes?

PEVERAL. Sorry, I only play for money.

DERBY DAN. Fair enough. Shall we say a pair to open?

PEVERAL. I told you, I don't play for food! Comprende?

DERBY DAN. Two of a kind, then?

PEVERAL. Sounds fair enough. *(PEVERAL starts dealing the cards.)*

DERBY DAN. Where's your ante?

PEVERAL. Back in Boston with my uncle, why?

DERBY DAN. *(Throwing the cards down.)* Never mind! I don't believe I've introduced myself yet. *(He takes out a Wanted poster of himself from inside his jacket and hands it to Peveral. PEVERAL is still dealing the cards to excess.)* And pour yourself a drink on me.

PEVERAL. I'm ameenable. *(PEVERAL starts pouring himself a drink with one hand and holds the poster up to read with the other. After a few seconds the liquor spills out onto the table as he continues to stare at the poster frozen in his hand.)*

DERBY DAN. *(Taking the bottle from his hand.)* Liquorin's mighty expensive to be spillin' like that. But I'm gonna do you a favor. I'm goin' to arrange it so you won't have to pay the bill - this time - or any other time!

PEVERAL. *(In a hushed tone.)* Say ... listen, Derby Dan. I wasn't really gonna do you any harm. I was just play-

cting to impress my girl. And I know there's no reason why you should, but if you could just play along and back down, I'd make it worth your while.

DERBY DAN. *(Shoving his chair back, gets up, grabs Peveral.)* Why you little... *(FARGO CALLAHAN steps out on the landing. DERBY DAN sees him, but Peveral's back is to him. DERBY puts his hands up.)* ...Derby Dan Turner. Please don't shoot me!

PEVERAL. *(Drawing near to him.)* That's great! But just a little more grovelling.

DERBY DAN. Oh, I'm in for it now! Jesus, Joseph and

Mary, I'm going to meet me maker!

PEVERAL. *(loudly)* Where do you want it, you mangy mealybug?

DERBY DAN. Oh, whatever will my poor wife and children do without me!

PEVERAL. *(drawing near again)* Hey, you don't have to ham it up.

FARGO. *(starts down the step)* Derby Dan Turner!

PEVERAL. Great, now you're a ventriloquist! Just stick to your part, will you? *(FARGO taps Peveral on the shoulder, and PEVERAL turns.)*

FARGO.
Alright, Derby Dan. Drop your gun on the floor.
I'm Fargo Callahan. Don't think we've met before.
(PEVERAL does so. LUCY drops behind the table.)

PEVERAL. The Rhyming Cowboy?

FARGO. At last we meet, Mr. Derby Dan Turner.

PEVERAL. Now don't get carried away, Callahan. There's been a slight mistake...

FARGO. The mistakes have all been on your side, Derby Dan. I'm taking you in, so that this territory will once again be safe for decent folks to live peaceably in. So that honest men can make an honest living ... and so that women folk can feel safe and free from the danger of being assaulted by the likes of your kind.

(LUCY pops from behind the table with her derringer, holds it to the back of his head.)

LUCY. Hold it right there, mister! Now drop it!

FARGO. Of course, some women take matters in their own hands. *(HE drops his gun. PEVERAL picks up his.)*

LUCY. Now hands up. *(FARGO puts his hands up.)*

PEVERAL. Thanks Lucy. Now, let's saddle up the horses and...

LUCY. *(to FARGO)* You aren't takin' in Derby Dan Turner without a fair fight. *(Picks up FARGO'S gun.)* Isn't that right, Derby Dan?

PEVERAL. Lucy, could I speak to you for a moment?

FARGO. Very clever, miss. But there's one thing you didn't take into account.

LUCY. Oh? What?

FARGO. My faithful Indian companion, Talking Boar, has you covered from behind.

LUCY. You expect me to believe that?

(TALKING BOAR enters from behind her, with a bow and arrow.)

TALKING BOAR. There is a grain of truth in what he says. Prudence dictates that you drop your weapon. *(EVERYBODY drops their guns. FARGO picks his up.)*

FARGO. Good work, Talking Boar.

TALKING BOAR. Yes, I believe it was one of Wellington's favorite military maxims that went, "Always watch your backside." With all due respect to the lady, *(Looking her up and down.)* ...the man was a genius.

(ELEANOR comes into view, getting the drop on TALKING BOAR with a rifle.)

ELEANOR. Hands up, Injun! *(THEY drop their guns and put their hands up.)* I knew you were nothing but a savage!

Assaulting innocent women.

TALKING BOAR. But that innocent woman had a gun.

(AMBROSE comes into view, putting a rifle at Eleanor's back.)

AMBROSE. And so do I! Alright! Drop it!

ELEANOR. *(Dropping her gun, turns around.)* Ambrose!

AMBROSE. *(embarrassed)* Oh, sorry, darling. I guess I got carried away.

PEVERAL. Excuse me, are my hands up or down now?

(THATAWAY comes into view holding a rifle.)

THATAWAY JACK. I think everybody's hands should be up. Except you, Pete. You're the only harmless one in here. *(EVERYONE looks to see who he's talking about. PEVERAL keeps his hands up and looks too.)* Put your hands down, Pete. No longer any use to play this game. You could get yourself hurt something awful. Why, you're gentler than a newborn fawn and as soft as a piece of molasses candy sitting in the sun. *(EVERYBODY looks around again, including PEVERAL.)* PUT 'EM DOWN, PETE. *(PEVERAL reluctantly does so.)*

LUCY. But that's Derby Dan Turner! The meanest, toughest man this side of the Pecos. The man I want to marry! *(PEVERAL puts his hands back up.)*

THATAWAY JACK. *(Slapping his hands back down.)* I think it's time you 'fess up, Pete.

PEVERAL. Oh, all right. Lucy, I'm not Derby Dan Turner at all.

Lucy. You're not? *(PEVERAL shakes his head.)* But you said you planted the Carnation Kid?

Peveral. I couldn't plant a tulip.

Lucy. And polishing off Silver Gun Sam?

Peveral. I never polished a doorknob.

Lucy. And you never ploughed down the Farmer Brothers?

Peveral. Lucy, I'm just not good with my hands!

Lucy. Well if you aren't Derby Dan Turner, who are you?

Peveral. Peveral Sommerset Biddingwell.

Lucy. Peveral! What are you doing here? Why did you pretend like this?

Peveral. I guess I figured it was the only way I could win you back. *(Pointing to Derby Dan.)* That's Derby Dan Turner. That's the man you love.

(PEVERAL fades back upstage.)

Thataway Jack. And that's the man you're looking for, Fargo. *(Picks up a gun and puts it in Derby Dan's holster.)* I believe, you two have some unfinished business together. *(Picks up another gun and puts it in Fargo's holster.)* I aim to make this a fair fight. So square off. *(THEY do so.)* On the count of three, draw. One ... two ...

Fargo. Wait a minute!

Thataway Jack. Now what?

Fargo. In the interest of law and order, I'm willing to take Derby Dan alive and let a jury of his peers decide his fate.

THATAWAY JACK. You hear that, Derby Dan? You can go quietly.

LUCY. He'll die first! Derby Dan Turner would never be taken alive!!

DERBY DAN. *(Looks at LUCY, then asks nobody in particular.)* Who is this girl?

THATAWAY JACK. Then you won't go quietly?

DERBY DAN. Well...

LUCY. You bet he won't! *(DERBY glares at her.)*

THATAWAY JACK. Alright then, you have your answer, Fargo. Now, on the count of three. One ... two ...

DERBY DAN. Wait a minute!

THATAWAY JACK. Now what is it?!

DERBY DAN. There's something in what the young girl says, but why mess up this lovely new establishment? I suggest we make an appointment to settle this out of town.

FARGO. Yes. At a more convenient time, perhaps?

DERBY DAN. Yeah. Tomorrow suit you?

FARGO. Suits me fine. After lunch?

THATAWAY JACK. Now wait a minute! While you're at it you might just as well pack a picnic basket! Now I'm counting for the last time. One ... two ...

FARGO. Hold it! I can't go through with this.

THATAWAY JACK. Why not?

FARGO. *(Dropping the FARGO CALLAHAN facade.)* Because I'm not the man you think I am.

THATAWAY JACK. You're not Fargo Callahan?

FARGO. Not really, Sir. No. There is no Fargo Callahan. There's only the legend. Fargo Callahan is a literary fiction. A paper creation of an eastern publishing company.

THATAWAY JACK. Then why all the get up?

FARGO. In the fiction business it pays to keep legends alive. The publishers pay me to go from town to town posing for pictures and spreading the word of my exploits in an effort to increase book sales.

THATAWAY JACK. Why would a man want to do such a thing?

FARGO. Well the pay is good, and I travel a great deal, people respect me...

AMBROSE. You mean they give you free accommodations!?

FARGO. I am sorry about that.

THATAWAY JACK. What about the Injun?

FARGO. Talking Boar isn't really my faithful Indian companion.

ELEANOR. He's a savage and a thief!

FARGO. Close. He's my agent.

TALKING BOAR. I resent that! However, it's true.

THATAWAY JACK. Well cut off both my legs and call me shorty. The stories I heard. It's been said that Fargo Callahan could shoot a bug off a bear's backside ridin' sidesaddle on a wild stallion!

FARGO. Say, that's good! (starts memorizing it) Shoot a bug...

THATAWAY JACK. And Talking Boar. I heard he could track the footprints of a flea in a sandstorm by the light of a wet match!

TALKING BOAR. (tries to memorize it) Track a flea sidesaddle...

FARGO. No no. That's mine.

THATAWAY JACK. Well I'm ashamed! 'Shamed and

slackjawed at the spectacle you two make. Much as I detest a man of Derby Dan's reputation, least I can appreciate the fact he's a man of his own making!

DERBY DAN. Thanks for the kind words, old-timer. And now if you'll all excuse me, I've got some business to take care of. *(starts to leave)*

THATAWAY JACK. Wait a minute. Just 'cause I admire the cut of your clothes, don't mean we come from the same tailor. Ain't none of us safe with you on the loose. so I guess it's up to me. Now draw, you no good...

PEVERAL. No, Thataway. this isn't your fight. It's mine. Hand me my gun.

THATAWAY JACK. But Pete, you can't use that gun...

PEVERAL. *(With hitherto unknown force.)* I said give me the gun, Thataway!

THATAWAY JACK. It's your funeral, Pete. *(Hands him the gun.)*

PEVERAL. Derby Dan, I always think it's fitting that a man knows what he's gettin' tangled up in. See that knot hole in the wall? I'm shootin' five rounds through that hole. The sixth bullet I'm saving for your belly.

(HE fires five shots.)

TALKING BOAR. I say, not bad. All five straight through.

PEVERAL. *(to Derby Dan)* Now draw, you pesky polecat!

FARGO. Sorry, that's mine. I used that epithet in *The Rhyming Cowboy Rides,* Doubleday, 1864.

PEVERAL. Well ... draw you yellow-bellied sidewinder!

FARGO. Sorry. *The Rhyming Cowboy Rides Again.* 1865.

PEVERAL. *(thinks a moment)* Draw, you weasle-headed wart-hog!

TALKING BOAR. Well, it's original, anyway.

DERBY DAN. No it isn't! I coined that sobriquet in *Derby Destroys Denver,* 1863, Putnam Press. *(EVERYONE looks to him. HE shrugs, sticks his hands in his pocket, smiles benignly, and drops the Derby Dan accent.)* Guess shootouts aren't really *my* line either.

THATAWAY JACK. What? Two make-believe legends?

DERBY DAN. I'm afraid so.

THATAWAY JACK. But there's a poster out on you.

DERBY DAN. Put up by the publishing company.

LUCY. Then there is no Derby Dan Turner!?

DERBY DAN. Sorry to disappoint you.

FARGO. *(to Derby Dan)* Say, Derby Dan, seeing the way things turned out, how about we go over to the saloon and I'll tell you about the latest Fargo Callahan book?

DERBY DAN. Don't mind if I do. Am I in it? *(THEY start out the front, with TALKING BOAR following.)*

FARGO. Chapter five. I stop you from terrorizing a family of Sheepherders, we shoot it out, and you narrowly escape by holding a young girl hostage at gunpoint.

DERBY DAN. Sounds rather far-fetched, if you ask me. How are sales?

TALKING BOAR. It's on the Best Seller List. Number seven and climbing. *(THEY are gone.)*

LUCY. Well, just imagine. Fakers. Nothing but fakers.

PEVERAL. *(with a touch of sarcasm)* Don't give up hope, Lucy. I'm sure if you look hard enough you can find someone to fulfill all your fantasies. *(heading upstairs)* I'm gonna change and pack my things, Thataway.

THATAWAY JACK. One thing, Pete. That was a nice trick you pulled with the gun full of blanks. But if he'd have called your bluff you'd have met your maker sure!

PEVERAL. Well, at least I would have died with my boots on. *(HE exits.)*

THATAWAY JACK. I was wrong about Pete, that's a fact. He's the bravest man I ever knowed.

AMBROSE. Excuse me, but may we put our hands down now?

THATAWAY JACK. Oh, sure. Go on about your business.

ELEANOR. *(As THEY exit.)* I'm going back to Daddy. On the next train out of here.

AMBROSE. *(overlapping)* Now Eleanor ... Darling ... *(AMBROSE and ELEANOR exit.)*

LUCY. Why would Peveral do that? With the blank gun?

THATAWAY JACK. *(Moving with LUCY to a table.)* Pete loves you Lucy, and I don't blame him. The Lord done give you two extra helpings of pretty and he weren't stingy with the side trimmings neither. You're dressed up better than a holiday turkey and you nearly smell as good.

LUCY. Peveral's never said anything like that to me.

THATAWAY JACK. Pete's shy, is all. He says your eyes sparkle like a breechloader going off on a clear summer night and your hands is as soft as stewed buffalo tongue.

LUCY. Peveral said that? Are you sure?

THATAWAY JACK. Sure I'm sure. Say, where'd you get all these notions about the west?

LUCY. *(Pulls a well-worn paperback from her purse.)* Here. Can everything in this book be a lie?

THATAWAY JACK. *(Reading with great difficulty.)* Ho-mer Good-stock; Jour-Jour-Journals of a Front-tiers-man. Now I see the trouble Pete's been having. Why you traipse about the prairie with the unsartin' footing of a three-legged horse. Lucy, these is just a lot of whipped-up bar tales. A few embers of truth blowed hot by some windbag. You seen how it was with Derby Dan and Fargo. Ain't you learned nothin' from what's happened here?

LUCY. Are you saying Peveral is different?

THATAWAY JACK. I'm a saying you shouldn't shuck Pete like a husk of corn cause he don't claim to be half gator and half mountain lion. We live in a world that's got no more permanence than a spider web in a wind blown cayon. The winds is coming from the east. They brought you and Pete and they'll bring thousands more like ya. You'll change the way rivers flow and the way mountains look. Mesquite that's growed for a thousand years will give way by the square mile, and my kind won't find no shade except as what's provided by mortgages and collaterals.

LUCY. That's beautiful!

THATAWAY JACK. *(considers)* Ain't bad at that. *(gets up)* Guess I'll go saddle the horses. Talk to Pete, Lucy. You might like what you hear.

(THATAWAY exits. PEVERAL comes downstairs dressed in his normal clothing.)

PEVERAL. Where's Thataway?

LUCY. He went to saddle up the horses.

PEVERAL. Oh. Well, I'll give him a hand. *(moves toward exit)*

LUCY. Wait a minute. *(HE stops.)* You know I've never really seen you before. You never sent me a picture.

PEVERAL. Nothing much to interest you. Just a banker, Lucy.

LUCY. Where do you go from here?

PEVERAL. Nowhere exciting. A little two-story red brick bank.

LUCY. I think I'd like to see that bank, Peveral. Can I come with you?

PEVERAL. *(Determined to have some pride.)* No, Lucy. I'd want to save you the embarrassment of telling your friends that the only thing I can lick is an envelope! *(SHE kisses him on the cheek.)* That the only thing I fill full of lead is my pencil!! *(SHE kisses him on the mouth.)* That the only way I settle an account is with a rubber stamp!!! *(SHE kisses him on the mouth and they hold for a few seconds.)* I still have the marriage license, Lucy.

LUCY. We could get married this afternoon. and be on our honeymoon tonight, if you have any interest...

PEVERAL. I'm a banker, Lucy.

LUCY. Care to make an investment?

(THEY kiss. THATAWAY comes back on.)

THATAWAY JACK. Well, I'm all set to go. Oh, 'scuse me. *(THEY break apart.)*

PEVERAL. Thataway, I've decided to stay here awhile.

THATAWAY JACK. Well, I figured as much.

PEVERAL. Am I that predictable?

THATAWAY JACK. That's a fact, Pete. Once I got a gander at Miss Lucy, here, I figured you was done fer. *(smiling)* I'll bet there ain't a tattoo on her body.

(AMBROSE and ELEANOR enter carrying packed suitcases.)

ELEANOR. Hurry along, Ambrose, or we'll miss our train.

AMBROSE. *(Handing THATAWAY a set of keys.)* Lock the place up when you leave. *(They start to go.)*

THATAWAY JACK. Whoooa! Where you headed off to?

ELEANOR. Cleveland. We've had quite enough of the Wild West.

AMBROSE. I'm already $20 in the red. Couple of more customers and I'm bankrupt. *(twitches)*

THATAWAY JACK. Things can't be as bad as all that. Didn't you hear my speech about the spider web in a wind-blown canyon?

AMBROSE. We missed that one.

THATAWAY JACK. We live in a world that's got no more permanence than a spider web...

AMBROSE. I lied! I lied! I heard it from the other room. But it doesn't change our minds.

THATAWAY JACK. How about this fifty dollars? That do anything for you? Thataway Jack always pays his bills. *(AMBROSE looks unmoved.)* I'm getting old, boy. My time is passing, but you folks are young, and the west needs your kind. Just like a tree that's first gotta shed its leaves before it can bear any new ones...

AMBROSE. *(Quickly taking the fifty dollars.)* We'll take it! We'll take it!

PEVERAL. Thataway, you nearly killed me for that fifty dollars!

THATAWAY JACK. *(winks at Peveral)* Take some of that money and give these young folks your best honeymoon suite. *(to Ambrose)* What do you say?

AMBROSE. I guess we could give it another try. How about it, Eleanor?

ELEANOR. Oh well ... I suppose so, Ambrose.

AMBROSE. Let's get this fifty dollars in the safe. *(HE exits, ELEANOR picks up her suitcases, and twitches.)*

ELEANOR. Uh oh. *(twitches)* Ambrose? *(twitches)* Ambrose! *(Hurries out after him.)*

PEVERAL. But Thataway, what about yourself? How will you get by?

THATAWAY JACK. Same as ever, Pete. A prairie man don't need much in the way of physical comforts. I'll get by. With the sky as my roof, the stars as my company and that bag of gold in my pocket. *(chuckles)*

PEVERAL. Wait a minute. You sold me the gold.

THATAWAY JACK. I guess I'm smarter than you look, Pete. That weren't real gold.

PEVERAL. Fool's gold?

THATAWAY JACK. *(chuckling)* No offense, Pete, but I figured I had me just the right person to try it out on.

LUCY. Where will you go, Thataway?

THATAWAY JACK. I won't be far, miss. Why every spring if you cock your ears toward them mountains and listen real careful, you'll hear the sound of rushing water as it makes its way down into the valley below and you can say, "Why, it's Thataway Jack! He's up there a'splashing around. And he ain't never really left me .. *(LUCY & PEVERAL start to embrace.)* ... Ain't never really left me a'tall." I'll be around, Pete. Where the grass is long and the mountains is tall, that's where I'll be. *(HE starts to head out, as the LOVERS try to embrace, stops.)* Wherever the fish bite more than the mosquitos, that's where I'll be. *(same business)* Wherever a man is free to sit peaceable like and listen to the coyote a singing him a song, that's where I'll be. *(HE exits. PEVERAL and LUCY look at one another. THEY finally embrace and kiss, as THATAWAY comes back for one more word.)* 'Course first I might make a stop in Denver. There's a lot of quality ladies up thataway!

(THATAWAY exits laughing. PEVERAL and LUCY kiss, as the LIGHTS...)

BLACKOUT
END OF PLAY

PROPERTY PLOT

PROLOGUE SCENE 1
Campfire unit
Coffee pot & cup
Stew pot
Bedroll (Blanket w/rope)
Canteen
Saddlebags
Rifle (Thataway)
Small tintype (Peveral)
Bag of golddust (Thataway)
Fifty dollars (Peveral)

SCENE 2
4 Place settings of china, crystal and silver (2 on each table)
4 Cloth napkins (tables)
Cash box (desk)
Hotel registration book (desk)
Desk blotter & pen set (desk)
Service bell (desk)
Spittoon (next to desk)
Stationery (desk)
Newspapers — 2 (behind desk)
Vases w/flowers on table
Lace tablecloths
A rather ornate, but battered chandelier
Bowie knife w/sheath (Talking Boar)
Indian pouch (Talking Boar)
Small hand-held barometer (Talking Boar)
Wanted posters (2, identical, 1 depicting Derby Dan, 1 Peveral) (Thataway Jack)

Wooden matches (Peveral)
Two-gun holster in white and guns (Fargo)
Indian beads (Fargo)
Holster and gun (Peveral)
Tom-toms (Offstage)
Bedsheets & blankets
Coins (Ambrose)
Serving tray (Eleanor)
Flask (Ambrose)
Derringer (Lucy)
Menus, 3, small
Plate (w/beef jerky & potatoes)
Plate (w/beef jerky only)
Coat (preset in closet—shot full of holes)
Pipe (Talking Boar)
Brandy snifter (Talking Boar)
Broken feather (Talking Boar)
Broken brandy snifter (Talking Boar)
Small period handbag w/arrow stuck through it (Lucy)
Dime novels (2)
Bottle of whiskey
2 Glasses
Deck of cards (Derby Dan Turner)
Black holster and gun (Derby Dan Turner)
Saddlebags (Derby Dan Turner)
Bow & arrow (Talking Boar)
Gun (Eleanor)
Rifle (Ambrose)
Handkerchief (Lucy)
2 Suitcases (Ambrose & Eleanor)
Keys (Ambrose)

IMPORTANT PROP NOTE

It has been discovered that one functional gun that shoots blanks can be passed between the three characters who need to shoot onstage. A second blank gun is needed only once, just after Derby Dan has used the gun onstage, during one of Fargo's exits it is necessary to have someone offstage fire some shots. All other prop guns need not be functional.

COSTUME PLOT

PEVERAL: At top of show and at close: Conservative period three-piece suit, dusty, with conservative dark bowler hat, wing-tip collar white shirt, bow tie or string tie. As Derby Dan Turner: outfit similar to actual Derby Dan, but a little off — red bandana, or slightly odd-looking bowler.

THATAWAY JACK: At top of show: dusty distressed prospector's hat, bulky hide and fringe mid-thigh jacket, red neck bandana, red flannel long-sleeve undershirt, worn blue denim jeans, leather chaps and boots. Later, remove jacket.

ELEANOR: Top of show: Teal colored, period floor-length skirt (slight train) with high-necked, lacy white blouse with French lacy bib-front apron, Gibson Girl hairdo. Add matching leg-o'mutton-sleeve travelling jacket.

AMBROSE: Top of show: White shirt with wing-tip collar, black string tie, arm garter, yellow and black plaid checked vest, dark straight leg trousers, spectacles. Add period teal colored jacket and dark hat.

TALKING BOAR: At top of show: fringed buckskin Indian shirt, v-cut in front to show some chest. Buckskin pants with fringe, buckskin knee-high lace-up boots. All with subtle Indian decoration, beads, bear claws, etc. Single feather and leather thong headdress, small leather pouch, bowie knife. Slight war paint on face and chest. Add: White chiffon cravat and satin mid-thigh tie-waist smoking jacket.

FARGO CALLAHAN: White fancy cowboy shirt and white pants trimmed with silver sequins, white cowboy boots, white hip gun holsters, white neck scarf, white cowboy hat.

LUCY: Top of show: long, dusty, period, woman's travelling coat or cloak to disguise brightly colored dance hall dress with slit to reveal a leg with thigh garter and rip-away section of cloth in back, period boots. Small, period handbag with arrow stuck through it.

DERBY DAN TURNER: White shirt w/no collar, black vest, black trousers, black boots, black neck-scarf, black derby, black glove on gun hand, black gun hip holster, long black coat.

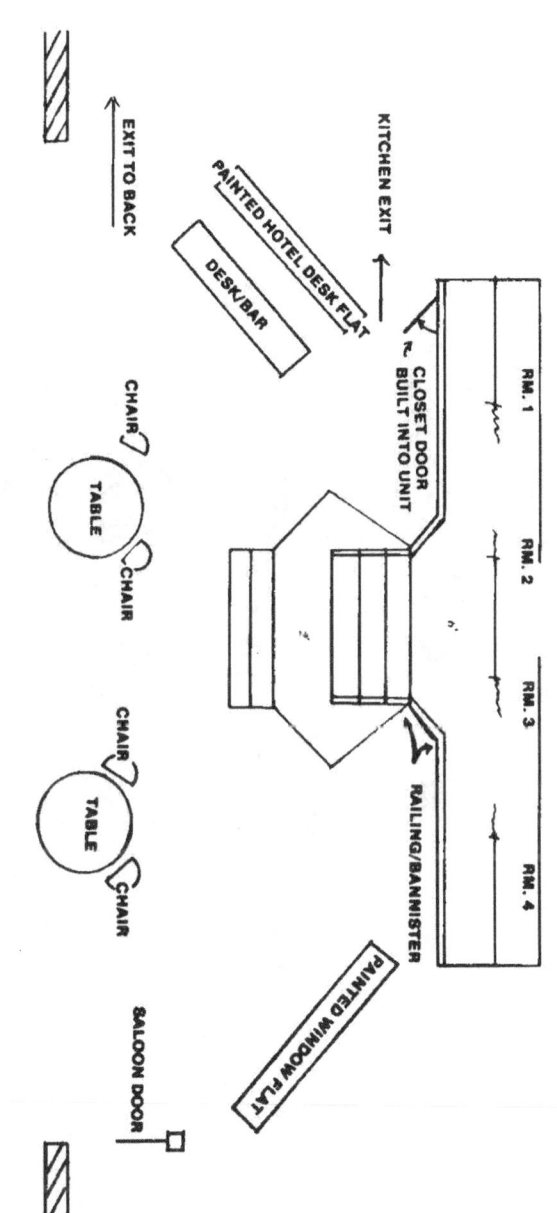

SET DESIGN
THATAWAY JACK
MAIN SET

EXIT TO BACK

PAINTED HOTEL DESK FLAT

DESK/BAR

KITCHEN EXIT

CLOSET DOOR
BUILT INTO UNIT

RM. 1

RM. 2

RM. 3

RM. 4

CHAIR

TABLE

CHAIR

CHAIR

TABLE

CHAIR

RAILING/BANNISTER

PAINTED WINDOW FLAT

SALOON DOOR

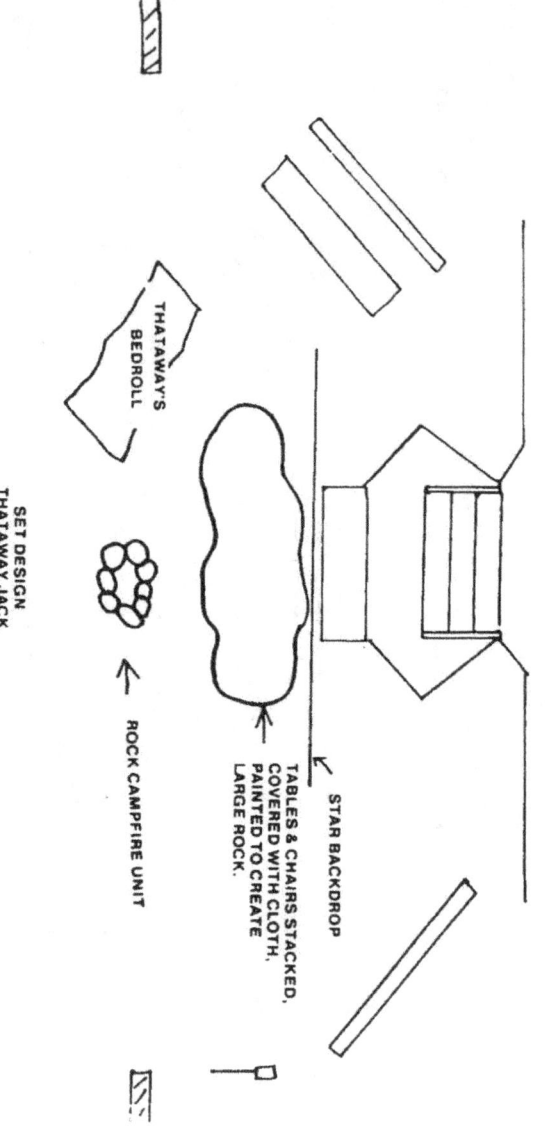

SET DESIGN
THATAWAY JACK
PROLOGUE

THATAWAY'S
BEDROLL

ROCK CAMPFIRE UNIT

TABLES & CHAIRS STACKED,
COVERED WITH CLOTH,
PAINTED TO CREATE
LARGE ROCK.

STAR BACKDROP